5E1

For my lovely Mumpy
SH xx

First published 2018 by Macmillan Children's Books
an imprint of Pan Macmillan
20 New Wharf Road, London N1 9RR
Associated companies throughout the world
www.panmacmillan.com

ISBN 978-1-5098-2745-9 (HB)
ISBN 978-1-5098-2746-6 (PB)
ISBN 978-1-5098-9482-6 (Ebook)

1 3 5 7 9 8 6 4 2

A CIP catalogue record for this book is available from
the British Library.

Printed in China

Sue Hendra & Paul Linnet

Snowball

MACMILLAN CHILDREN'S BOOKS

Miles up, all alone
on a hill, looking down

a little round snowball
gazed towards town.

It looked so exciting,
he wanted to play,
it was time for some fun
and today was the day.

If he stayed where he was
in the high mountain air
he'd have no one to play with
and that isn't fair!

He made up his mind
to go on a mission . . .
the town would be fun,
he had a suspicion.

So off Snowball set
with a, "Jiggy, jig jig!"

But he didn't catch sight of
a pesky brown twig.

That pesky old twig
caused Snowball to stumble,

the poor little fellow
had taken a tumble.

As he skidded
and bounced
what he didn't
yet know

was that as he
rolled downwards

he'd pick up
more snow.

And as he rolled faster
with grace and with vigour
he started to grow...

getting bigger

and bigger.

He was picking up snow,
bits and bobs, this and that . . .

Pebble nose,

sticky arms,

and a sheep for a . . .

HAT!

"Ooops!" said the snowball,
"but what can I do?"
"Baaaa!" cried the sheep
who was stuck on like glue.

More snow piled on
as he carried on growing,
faster and faster —
no sign of him slowing.

He was boinging and bouncing
down, down, down,
crashing and spinning,
heading for town.

Rabbits and flowers were in for a squashing,
and now he was heading for somebody's washing!

Tumbling and twirling
faster and faster.
Oh, my goodness —
What a disaster!

Some spectacles here,

some sausages there,

Romantic couples
out for a meal,

The Mayor of the town?
Not her Ladyship too!

and no
Snowball, no . . .
Please don't visit the

dozens of dogs,

and a big scary bear!

an acrobat team,

an electric eel!

ZOO!

Squawking and roaring, growling and hooting,
croaking and hissing, screeching and tooting!

The snowball was zooming as fast as a rocket,
filling with stuff like a gigantic pocket.

Zigging and zagging
down, down, down,
bashing and smashing
through the small town.

Still gathering snow
he shot past in a flash
then, all of a sudden,
an almighty...

. . . CRASH!

Out flew a pebble, some sticks and a sheep.
Out came some socks and some pants in a heap.
Sausages, dogs and a big scary bear,
a romantic couple with snow in their hair.
The acrobat team, the electric eel,
the Mayor of the town spinning out like a wheel.
And not to forget, the whole of the zoo,
the snowball had managed to swallow that too!

After all the commotion
the scene was snow white.
The end of the story?
Well, not yet, not quite . . .

Unlike the beginning,
as this story ends,
Our lonely young snowball
has made lots of . . .

FRIENDS!

Ooops!